All Things Purple!

Wait...what are purple things?

WRITTEN BY PRISCILA LOPEZ AND ILLUSTRATED BY ELVIS CAMARENA

For Penelope and Zaya

Purple **Whale?**

No probably not.
They're **Blue.**

Purple... ocean?

Doesn't seem likely.

They're **Blue** too!

Purple *grass?*

I believe the grass is green!

I Know!

Purple *Sheep!*

No, that does not seem right...

They are *white* and fluffy.

Purple **clouds.**

Yes, clouds!

Interesting, but nope.

They are *white.*

A Purple

Pineapple!

I LOVE pineapples!

Z, those are **yellow,** not purple.

A purple **giraffe!**

What about a *carrot...*

or a **PUMPKIN?** are they purple?

I have never seen a purple carrot or pumpkin...

They must be Orange.

Hmm... I am certain yummy strawberries are purpl

along with Flamingos!

Z, you have such an imagination!

Flamingos are *pink* and strawberries are *red!*

Then what are **Purple** things?

Well...

Grapes.

Flowers.

Hippos.

But thinking about it,

Purple can be anything you want...

When you

imagine purple

it becomes purple.

So, Imagine!

Great! 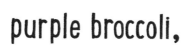 I see a...

purple broccoli,

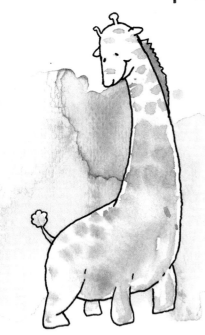

purple car,

purple giraffe,

purple...
Everything!

The End.

Made in the USA
Middletown, DE
19 October 2023

40354601R00018